BUNNIES
ALL DAY LONG

Pictures by Marie H. Henry
Story by Amy Ehrlich

Dial Books for Young Readers
E. P. Dutton, Inc. / *NEW YORK*

For my daughter Benedicte
M. H. H.

*For my wonderful
friends at Dial*
A. E.

First published in the United States 1985 by
Dial Books for Young Readers
A Division of E. P. Dutton, Inc.
2 Park Avenue
New York, New York 10016
Originally published by Duculot, Paris-Gembloux 1985
Published simultaneously in Canada by
Fitzhenry & Whiteside Limited, Toronto
©1985 by Duculot Paris-Gembloux
©1985 by Amy Ehrlich for the American text
All rights reserved

Printed in Belgium by Offset Printing Van den Bossche
Typography by Atha Tehon
First Edition
COBE
10 9 8 7 6 5 4 3 2 1

Library of Congress in Publication Data
Henry, Marie.
Bunnies all day long.
Summary: Mischievous bunny children Harry, Larry,
and Paulette have a busy day at home and at school.
1. Children's stories, French. [1. Rabbits—Fiction.]
I. Ehrlich, Amy, 1942– . II. Title.
PZ7.H3932Bu 1985 [E] 84-20031
ISBN 0-8037-0185-3

The art for each picture consists of a watercolor painting,
which is camera-separated and reproduced in full color.

In the bunny family nothing ever went smoothly. That was because there were two bunny brothers and an older bunny sister who were always getting into trouble.

Poor Mother Bunny had only a few moments of peace and quiet each morning before she went to wake her children.

Larry and Harry, the bunny brothers, looked so sweet when they were sleeping. Mother Bunny wished she didn't have to get them out of bed. But it was a school day and it was getting late.

"Rise and shine," said Mother Bunny. "Time to get dressed."

Meanwhile Paulette, the older bunny sister, was
still asleep. Larry and Harry wouldn't stand for that.
"Wake up or we'll tickle your toes," they shouted.

But at bathtime Paulette had a chance to get even.

"You're getting soap in my eyes," said Harry. "I want Mama to wash me."

"Too hot!" said Larry.

"Too bad!" said Paulette.

Things went from bad to worse at breakfast.
"Carrot flakes again?" complained Harry.
"But carrot flakes are good for you," said Paulette.
Larry was too busy eating to say anything at all.

The bunny children were about to be late for school.

Paulette was the last one ready. That's because Larry and Harry had borrowed her slicker and left it outside in the garden.

"Now stay together and don't forget to keep your rain hats on," said Mother Bunny.

"Wait for me!" shouted Paulette. "I'm coming!"
The wind howled and the rain poured down as the
bunny children raced each other to school.

"Hurry, hurry!" said the teacher.

"One carrot plus two carrots is how many carrots?" asked the teacher in the arithmetic lesson.

"Who cares," mumbled Paulette. "I'd rather eat carrots than count them."

"Use your head, you dumb bunny. It's easy," said Larry.

Poor Paulette. Everyone was picking on her.

She went into the corner and cried. Maybe she'd stay there forever. Then they'd be sorry for being so mean.

It was time for recess. Larry, the daredevil, slid down the banister. But there was a surprise waiting for him at the bottom.

"I'm coming! I'll rescue you!" yelled Harry.

Next Larry swung from a trapeze in the rafters.
"Look at me," said Harry. "I can stand on my hands."
"Not for long!" said Paulette, giving him a push.

But better than recess was the end of school with
Mother Bunny waiting. She had a hug for each of
them and a big red umbrella to keep away the rain.
"How was school?" she asked.

   "Paulette got in trouble in arithmetic," said Larry.

   "Don't be a tattletale," said Harry.

   "Tattletale, tattletale," echoed the raindrops.

As soon as they got home, the bunny children were ready for a snack.

"Here's the bread," said Larry.

"Here are the carrots," said Harry.

"Be careful," warned Paulette. "This isn't a ball game, you know."

"A ball game. What a great idea!" said Harry.

"Paulette may be smarter than she looks," said Larry. "Let's go get the soccer ball. She can be the goalie."

Uh-oh! The bunny children didn't know that Father Bunny was home from work. And they never meant to break Mother Bunny's jar, really they didn't.

"Come on, let's work fast," said Harry. "I want to see what we're having for dinner."

The kitchen was cozy and warm. It was the very best place to be when dinner was cooking. Mother Bunny caught Larry sneaking some radish pudding but only winked at him. After all, she was doing it herself!

"Something smells good," said Paulette. "Ah, turnip stew. I think I'll just stir it a bit." But when Mother Bunny asked them to set the table, Paulette was no longer so eager to help.

"Cooking's easy," said Harry.

"Just watch me flip this omelet...."

"I guess I missed. What a flop!"

"The food looks grand," said Father Bunny. "I really don't think we needed that omelet after all."

After dinner the bunny family sat comfortably together in the firelit room. Mother and Father Bunny hated to ask the children to go to bed because they were reading their book so quietly. Sure enough, as they were getting undressed, they began a tug-of-war.

"Mama, Mama," cried Larry. "We're ready to go to sleep. Come and kiss us good night."

"Yes, my little bunnies. And now to bed with you. Good night, good night, good night."